Music Player
STORYBOOK®

stories written by Farrah McDoogle
illustrations by Tom Brannon

Contents

 Our Favorite Animals 4

Food, Yummy Food! 12

It's Fun to Imagine 20

Fun with Friends 30

Reader's Digest
Children's Books®

New York, New York • Montréal, Québec • Bath, United Kingdom

Our Favorite Animals

"Hey Bert, of all the bugs and animals, what's your favorite?" Ernie wondered one day as the buddies looked around the park.

"Well, I don't know, Ernie," said Bert. "There sure are a lot to choose from—baboons and bears, even spiders, flies, and fleas."

"Don't forget dogs and squirrels...and even elephants," Ernie reminded him.

"All of those are great," Bert said. "But Bernice is definitely my favorite. None of those is as special as my Bernice, the perfect pigeon."

"You know, Bert, none of those is as special as Rubber Duckie either," Ernie answered. "He will always be my favorite."

Rubber Duckie

Lyrics and music by Jeff Moss

Rubber Duckie, you're the one.
You make bath time lots of fun.
Rubber Duckie,
I'm awfully fond of you.
Vo-vo dee-o.

Rubber Duckie, joy of joys,
when I squeeze you,
you make noise.
Rubber Duckie,
you're my very best friend,
it's true.

Oh, every day when I
make my way to the tubby,
I find a little fella who's
cute and yellow and chubby.
Rub-a-dub-dubby.

Rubber Duckie, you're so fine
and I'm lucky that you're mine.
Rubber Duckie, I'm
awfully fond of...
Rubber Duckie, I'm
awfully fond of you.

The Animal Fair

I went to the animal fair,
the birds and the beasts were there.
The big baboon,
by the light of the moon,
was combing his auburn hair.
The monkey bumped the skunk
and sat on the elephant's trunk.

The elephant sneezed
and fell to his knees,
and what became of the monk,
the monk, the monk, the monk,
the monk, the monk, the monk?

Play
Song 3

Eency-Weency Spider

Eency-weency spider
went up the waterspout.
Down came the rain
and washed the spider out.

Out came the sun
and dried up all the rain.
The eency-weency spider
went up the spout again.

7

Play Song 4

The Bear Went over the Mountain

The bear went over the mountain.
The bear went over the mountain.
The bear went over the mountain,
to see what he could see,
to see what he could see,
to see what he could see.

The other side of the mountain,
the other side of the mountain,
the other side of the mountain,
was all that he could see,
was all that he could see,
was all that he could see.
The other side of the mountain,
was all that he could see!

Old McDonald Had a Farm

Old McDonald had a farm,
E-I-E-I-O.
And on his farm he had a cow,
E-I-E-I-O.
With a *moo, moo* here,
and a *moo, moo* there.
Here a *moo*, there a *moo*,
everywhere a *moo, moo.*
Old McDonald had a farm,
E-I-E-I-O.

Old McDonald had a farm,
E-I-E-I-O.
And on his farm he had a pig,
E-I-E-I-O.
With an *oink, oink* here,
and an *oink, oink* there.
Here an *oink*, there an *oink*,
everywhere an *oink, oink.*
Old McDonald had a farm,
E-I-E-I-O.

Five Little Ducks

Five little ducks
went swimming one day,
over the pond and far away.
Mother Duck said,
"Quack, quack, quack, quack."
But only four little ducks
came back.

Four little ducks
went swimming one day,
over the pond and far away.
Mother Duck said,
"Quack, quack, quack, quack."
But only three little ducks
came back.

Three little ducks
went swimming one day,
over the pond and far away.
Mother Duck said,
"Quack, quack, quack, quack."
But only two little ducks
came back.

Two little ducks
went swimming one day,
over the pond and far away.
Mother Duck said,
"Quack, quack, quack, quack."
But only one little duck
came back.

One little duck
went swimming one day,
over the pond and far away.
Mother Duck said,
"Quack, quack, quack, quack."
But none of the five little ducks
came back.

Mother Duck
went swimming one day,
over the pond and far away.
Mother Duck said,
"Quack, quack, quack, quack."
And all of the five little ducks
came back!

Food, Yummy Food!

It was five minutes past lunchtime, and Cookie Monster's tummy was rumbling! "Me need nutrients, fast!" Cookie cried. In the kitchen he found apples and bananas, peas and corn, and one great, big roly-poly meatball.

"This food so yummy!" Cookie exclaimed between mouthfuls. "And healthy, too! How about that?"

Cookie's tummy stopped grumbling. "Me think me have room for one more food!" Cookie said, choosing a cookie—a great, big, crunchy cookie. "Since me eat so many healthy foods, it okay for me to have sometimes food like nice COOKIE!"

Finally, Cookie was full...until dinner time!

Play Song 1

C Is for Cookie

Lyrics and music by Joe Raposo

C is for cookie, that's good enough for me.
C is for cookie, that's good enough for me.
C is for cookie, that's good enough for me.
Oh, cookie, cookie, cookie starts with C.

Oh, C is for cookie, that's good enough for me.
C is for cookie, that's good enough for me.
C is for cookie, that's good enough for me.
Oh, cookie, cookie, cookie starts with C.

So, C is for cookie, that's good enough for me.
C is for cookie, that's good enough for me.
C is for cookie, that's good enough for me.
Oh, cookie, cookie, cookie starts with C.
Yeah, cookie, cookie, cookie starts with C.
Oh boy! Cookie, cookie, cookie starts with C.

Apples and Bananas

I like to eat, eat, eat apples and bananas.
I like to eat, eat, eat apples and bananas.

I like to ate, ate, ate ay-ples and bay-nay-nays.
I like to ate, ate, ate ay-ples and bay-nay-nays.

I like to eet, eet, eet ee-ples and bee-nee-nees.
I like to eet, eet, eet ee-ples and bee-nee-nees.

I like to ite, ite, ite i-ples and bi-ni-nis.
I like to ite, ite, ite i-ples and bi-ni-nis.

I like to ote, ote, ote o-ples and bo-no-nos.
I like to ote, ote, ote o-ples and bo-no-nos.

I like to oot, oot, oot oo-ples and boo-noo-noos.
I like to oot, oot, oot oo-ples and boo-noo-noos.

Sing a Song of Sixpence

Sing a song of sixpence,
a pocket full of rye;
four and twenty blackbirds
baked in a pie!

When the pie was opened,
the birds began to sing.
Wasn't that a dainty dish
to set before a king?

The Muffin Man

Oh, do you know the muffin man,
the muffin man, the muffin man?
Oh, do you know the muffin man
that lives on Drury Lane?

Oh, yes, I know the muffin man,
the muffin man, the muffin man.
Oh, yes, I know the muffin man
that lives on Drury Lane.

Polly, Put the Kettle On

Polly, put the kettle on,
Polly, put the kettle on,
Polly, put the kettle on,
we'll all have tea.

Sukey, take it off again,
Sukey, take it off again,
Sukey, take it off again,
they've all gone away.

Blow the fire and make the toast.
Put the muffins on to roast.
Blow the fire and make the toast,
we'll all have tea.

Play Song 6

Oats, Peas, Beans, & Barley Grow

Chorus:
Oats, peas, beans, and barley grow.
Oats, peas, beans, and barley grow.
Can you or I or anyone know
how oats, peas, beans, and barley grow?

Verse 1:
Thus the farmer sows the seed.
Thus he stands and takes his ease.
He stamps his foot and claps his hands,
and turns around and views the land. *(Chorus)*

Additional verses:
Next the farmer waters the seed, etc. *(Chorus)*
Next the farmer hoes the weeds, etc. *(Chorus)*
Last the farmer harvests the seed, etc. *(Chorus)*

It's Fun to Imagine

Whump, whump, whump! Elmo wonders if you have ever seen a helicopter in the sky. Whenever Elmo sees one, Elmo thinks about what Sesame Street would look like from there. How about we imagine that together?

Wow! Everything looks different from way up here! It's like the map on the wall at Elmo's school. Elmo sees trees and railroads. Look! Elmo can see the ocean. And there's Elmo's neighborhood! Do you see it? All the people look like itty-bitty dots, even big people, like firefighters. And the cars look like toy cars.

Pretending you're flying in a helicopter over your neighborhood is really fun, isn't it? But Elmo thinks it's more fun to be on the ground at home, because there's no better place to be!

People in Your Neighborhood

Lyrics and music by Jeff Moss

Oh, who are the people in your neighborhood,
in your neighborhood,
in your neighborhood?
Say, who are the people in your neighborhood,
the people that you meet each day?

Oh, the postman always brings the mail
through rain or snow or sleet or hail.
"I'll work and work the whole day through
to get your letter safe to you."

'Cause a postman is a person in your neighborhood,
in your neighborhood.
He's in your neighborhood.
A postman is a person in your neighborhood,
a person that you meet each day.

Oh, a fireman is brave, it's said.
His engine is a shiny red.
"If there's a fire anywhere about,
well, I'll be sure to put it out."

'Cause a fireman is a person in your neighborhood,
in your neighborhood.
He's in your neighborhood,
and a postman is a person in your neighborhood.
Well, they're the people that you meet
when you're walkin' down the street.
They're the people that you meet each day.

I've Been Working on the Railroad

I've been working on the railroad,
all the live-long day.
I've been working on the railroad,
just to pass the time away.
Don't you hear the whistle blowing?
Rise up so early in the morn.

Don't you hear the captain shouting
"Dinah, blow your horn"?

Chorus (sing twice):
Dinah, won't you blow,
Dinah, won't you blow,
Dinah, won't you blow your horn?

A Sailor Went to Sea

A sailor went to sea, sea, sea,
to see what he could see, see, see,
but all that he could see, see, see,
was the bottom of the deep blue sea, sea, sea.

Hey, Diddle Diddle

Hey, diddle diddle,
the cat and the fiddle,
the cow jumped over the moon.
The little dog laughed to see such sport
and the dish ran away with the spoon.

Down by the Bay

Down by the bay
where the watermelons grow,
back to my home
I dare not go.
For if I do,
my mother will say,
"Did you ever see a bear
combing his hair
down by the bay?"

Down by the bay
where the watermelons grow,
back to my home
I dare not go.
For if I do,
my mother will say,
"Did you ever see a whale
with a polka-dot tail
down by the bay?"

Fun with Friends

"Zoe, I really like your pink tutu!" said Abby. "It's sooo enchanting!"

"Ooooh, that made me feel all sunny inside," said Zoe. "I have an idea! Let's all say something nice. I'll go first."

The girls thought that was a great idea.

"Rosita, you dance salsa better than anyone on Sesame Street," Zoe said.

"Ooooh, you're right, Zoe, it feels like sunshine," said Rosita. "*Gracias, amiga.* My turn now! Abby, I love the way you sing. Zoe, your smile makes everybody happy."

"Thanks!" Zoe and Abby giggled together. "*Gracias, amiga.*"

"I have something to say about all of us!" said Abby. "We're great friends...and that's magical!"

Sesame Street Theme

Lyrics by Joe Raposo, Bruce Hart, and Jon Stone
Music by Joe Raposo

Sunny day
sweepin' the clouds away,
on my way to
where the air is sweet.
Can you tell me how to get,
how to get to Sesame Street?

Come and play!
Everything's A-OK.
Friendly neighbors there,
that's where we meet.
Can you tell me how to get,
how to get to Sesame Street?

It's a magic carpet ride.
Every door will open wide
to happy people like you.
Happy people like…
What a beautiful…

Sunny day
sweepin' the clouds away,
on my way to
where the air is sweet.
Can you tell me how to get,
how to get to Sesame Street?
How to get to Sesame Street?

If You're Happy and You Know It

If you're happy and you know it, clap your hands. *(Clap twice)*
If you're happy and you know it, clap your hands. *(Clap twice)*
If you're happy and you know it, then your face will surely show it!
If you're happy and you know it, clap your hands. *(Clap twice)*

If you're happy and you know it, stomp your feet. *(Stomp twice)*
If you're happy and you know it, stomp your feet. *(Stomp twice)*
If you're happy and you know it, then your face will surely show it!
If you're happy and you know it, stomp your feet. *(Stomp twice)*

Additional verses:
Shout, "Hooray" (Shout, "Hooray")
Do all three (Clap twice, stomp
twice, then shout, "Hooray")

Looby Loo

Chorus:
Here we go looby loo.
Here we go looby light.
Here we go looby loo,
all on a Saturday night.

Put your right hand in,
put your right hand out,
then give your right hand a
shake, shake, shake,
and turn yourself about.

(Repeat Chorus)

Additional verses:
Put your left hand in, etc.
Put your right foot in, etc.
Put your left foot in, etc.
Put your whole self in, etc.

34

A Little Wheel A-Turnin' in My Heart

There's a little wheel
a-turnin' in my heart.
There's a little wheel
a-turnin' in my heart,
in my heart,
in my heart.
There's a little wheel
a-turnin' in my heart.

Oh, I feel so very happy
in my heart.
Oh, I feel so very happy
in my heart.
In my heart,
in my heart;
oh, I feel so very happy
in my heart.

Rig-a-Jig

As I was walking
down the street,
Heigh-o, heigh-o,
heigh-o, heigh-o.
A pretty girl I chanced to meet.
Heigh-o, heigh-o, heigh-o.

Rig-a-jig-jig and away we go,
away we go, away we go.
Rig-a-jig-jig and away we go.
Heigh-o, heigh-o, heigh-o.